VIKING
Published by the Penguin Group
Penguin Books USA Inc., 375 Hudson Street, New York, New York 10014, U.S.A.
Penguin Books Ltd, 27 Wrights Lane, London W8 5TZ, England
Penguin Books Australia Ltd, Ringwood, Victoria, Australia
Penguin Books Canada Ltd, 10 Alcorn Avenue, Toronto, Ontario, Canada M4V 3B2
Penguin Books (N.Z.) Ltd, 182-190 Wairau Road, Auckland 10, New Zealand

Penguin Books Ltd, Registered Offices: Harmondsworth, Middlesex, England

First published in 1995 by Viking, a division of Penguin Books USA Inc.

1 3 5 7 9 10 8 6 4 2

Text copyright © Charles Black, 1995
Illustrations copyright © James Stevenson, 1995
All rights reserved

LIBRARY OF CONGRESS CATALOGING-IN-PUBLICATION DATA
Black, Charles C.
The royal nap / by Charles C. Black; illustrated by James Stevenson.   p.   cm.
Summary: Even the noise of a hiccup keeps King Gordo from falling asleep at naptime,
until he discovers the soothing effect of a sad song.
ISBN 0-670-85863-3
[1. Kings, queens, rulers, etc.—Fiction. 2. Naps (Sleep)—Fiction. 3. Noise—Fiction.] I. Stevenson, James.
II. Title.
PZ7.B52867Ro 1995 [E]—dc20   94-30728 CIP AC

Printed in Mexico   Set in Clearface

The
Royal
Nap

The great stone castle of King Gordo was a noisy place. Trumpets blew, flags flapped, armor clanked, doors slammed, swords fell over, plates crashed.

But every day at exactly one o'clock the castle suddenly became silent.

It was time for the Royal Nap.

"The king needs absolute quiet for his nap," said Lord Twombly, the king's assistant. "When His Majesty can't get to sleep, His Majesty gets cross."

Nobody in the castle wanted that to happen.

If the people in the castle had to go anywhere, they took off their boots and tiptoed around in their socks.

Then they waited, until at last they heard—echoing down the halls—the royal snore:

Awww . . . woga-oga-goga . . . onk.

4

Some days, the king never did fall asleep. His hearing was very sharp. One nap was spoiled by the sound of a moth landing in a room two doors away. Another day, he leapt from his bed and ran up and down the corridor in his nightgown, until he discovered one of the housekeepers dusting with a feather duster.

"Stop that racket!" cried the king. He snatched the feather duster and flung it out the window.

But a few weeks later, something much worse happened.

The king began to look tired all the time. His eyes were red, and he lost his temper over little things.

"Perhaps His Majesty is not getting enough rest," said Lord Twombly.

"Of course I'm not!" shouted the king. "The castle is too noisy! Do you hear me? Too noisy!"

That very afternoon, the king went to his room for the Royal Nap, slammed the door, and—moments later—opened it again. "Come here, Twombly!" he roared.

Lord Twombly came running. "Yes, Your Majesty?" he gasped.

"Hear that noise?" said the king.

Lord Twombly listened. "My ears are not as excellent as His Majesty's," said Lord Twombly. "I'm afraid I don't."

"There it is again!" said the king. "It goes *hic . . . hic . . . hic. . . .*"

"We shall search the castle," said Lord Twombly, "and find the noise immediately." He called out the palace guards, and they began the search.

The guards went up and down the many halls, out onto the parapets, up to the towers, listening. They heard nothing.

It was only when they crept down a set of dark and slippery stairs leading below the kitchen that they heard what they were searching for.

"*Hic . . . hic . . . hic . . .*"

In the dank, smelly dish-washing room, between two mountains of dirty pots and pans, sat Gerald, the old pot-scrubber, holding a dishcloth over his mouth. "I've got the hiccups," he said, "and I can't make them—*hic*—stop."

"The king is going to be very angry," said a guard named Sidney. "Have you tried holding your breath and swallowing a cupful of water?"

"Yes," said Gerald. "*Hic.*"

"How about a spoonful of sugar?" said a guard named Tom.

"That, too," said Gerald.

"Has anybody tried to startle you?" asked a guard named Ernst.

"Yes, but it didn't work," said Gerald. "Nothing—*hic*—works."

The guards carried Gerald up the stairs.

They took him before the king.

"Here is the culprit who disturbed the Royal Nap, Your Majesty," said Lord Twombly.

"Do you have anything to say for yourself?" said King Gordo.

"*Hic*," said Gerald. "Your Majesty."

"Banish him to the Cold and Snowy Land!" said King Gordo.

HIC
HIC
HIC

Gerald was put in a wagon and driven away from the castle. His friends waved sadly to him from the windows. "Try to keep warm, Gerald!" they called. "Take care of yourself." "Wear dry socks!"

Soon the last hiccup faded, and the wagon was gone. The workers returned to their washing and scrubbing and polishing.

But one person—a young plate-scraper named Phoebe—stayed at the window, watching and waving, long after Gerald was out of sight. Her tears rolled down her cheeks and splashed in the moat below.

PLINK

Gerald was put into a small cabin in the Cold and Snowy Land. He kept a fire going in the fireplace, and he cooked beans, and he slept on a pile of straw. It was lonely. The days and nights passed slowly. The only sounds were the wailing of the wind through the trees, the splinter of icicles falling on the frozen snow, and, of course, from the little cabin, the steady "*hic . . . hic . . . hic. . . .*"

The king's naps did not get any better. The king tossed and turned in his bed each day at one o'clock, twisting and squirming. He tried not to listen for any sounds. But when he didn't hear any, he started listening again for what he might have missed.

Every day, the people in the castle strained to hear the familiar *awww . . . woga-oga-goga . . . onk* from the king's room, but they didn't.

The king's eyes got redder, his temper got shorter, and all day long, he yawned.

One afternoon, while the king was rolling around in his bed, he heard a new noise.

The noise went *Plink . . . Plunk . . . Plink. . . .*

"Twombly!" yelled the king.

Twombly came running, and the guards were sent searching.
Again, it was only when they went with Twombly down the dark and slippery steps below the kitchen that they found the sound.

Plink . . . Plunk . . . Plink . . .

They peered into the dish-washing room. There was Phoebe, the plate-scraper, standing knee-deep in soap suds. In her hands was a broken old lute with a single string. Phoebe was plunking it and humming a soft tune.

Plink . . . Plunk . . . Plink . . .

"What do you think you're doing?" cried Twombly. "This is the Royal Nap Time!"

"Oh, my goodness," said Phoebe. "I forgot."

"Take her to the king," said Twombly.
When Phoebe was led before the king, he glared at her.
"Why did you make noise during my nap?" he demanded.

"I'm sorry, Your Majesty," said Phoebe. "I was writing a song and playing the lute."

"Song?" said the king. "What sort of a song?"

"A sad song," said Phoebe.

"Let's hear it," said the king.

Phoebe began to play the lute. *Plink . . . Plunk . . . Plink . . .*
Then she hummed a bit. The king gave a mighty yawn.

"I'm feeling very sad," sang Phoebe, "because—
Awww . . . woga-oga-goga . . . onk.
Phoebe's song was drowned out by the king's snoring.

"You've put His Majesty to sleep!" whispered Twombly. "I can't
believe it. He hasn't napped for weeks!" He sent Phoebe back to the
dish-washing room.

Two hours later, the king woke up. He looked around and smiled.
"I've just had the most wonderful nap," he said.

The next day, just before one o'clock, the king sent for Phoebe again. She climbed the dark and slippery stairs, carrying her broken lute.

"Play that song again," said the king.

Plink . . . Plunk . . . Plink . . . "I'm feeling very sad—" sang Phoebe.

Awww . . . woga-oga-goga . . . onk. The king was sound asleep again. This time he slept for three hours.

When he woke up, he danced a little dance. "I've never felt so good," he said.

The third day, Phoebe came upstairs again.

"Play it," said the king.

"No, Your Majesty," said Phoebe.

Twombly gasped.

"What?" said the king.

"I cannot play and sing anymore," she said.

"Of course you can," said the king. "I can't sleep without it."

"No, Your Majesty," said Phoebe again.

"What's wrong?" said Twombly to Phoebe.

"I'll tell you," said Phoebe. "It's what my song is about."

Phoebe picked up the lute. "I'm feeling very sad," she sang, "because my father is banished to the Cold and Snowy Land."

"Gerald, the pot-scrubber?" said Twombly.

"That fellow with the hiccups?" said the king.

"Yes," said Phoebe. "And I will not play or sing until my father returns."

"This is nonsense," said Twombly. "How dare you tell the king what to do?"

"What about my nap?" moaned the king. "I want my nap."

"I'll be glad to sing and play," said Phoebe, "the minute my father sets foot back in the castle."

Gerald was sitting in his cabin, listening to the wind and hiccuping, when there was a knock at the door. He was so startled he jumped into the air. "Who is it?" he cried.

"It's Lord Twombly," said a voice. "The king has forgiven you. I have come to take you back to the castle."

Gerald opened the door. He saw Lord Twombly and, behind him, a fancy carriage with eight horses.

"How are your hiccups?" said Twombly.

"Hiccups?" said Gerald. He suddenly realized he was not hiccuping. "I guess you scared them out of me," he said, and he followed Twombly to the carriage.

When Gerald returned to the castle, King Gordo gave him a better job—Royal Flag-Folder, which was quite easy to do, and meant that he got plenty of fresh air—and his daughter Phoebe was given a new job, too. She became His Majesty's Song-Singer, and she played the lute at nap time and sang until the king fell asleep.

AWWW WOGA OGA GOGA ONK

After that, every day the castle echoed from one o'clock to three o'clock with the royal snore: ***Awww . . . woga-oga-goga . . . onk. Awww . . . woga-oga-goga . . . onk.***

And Phoebe's job gave her plenty of time off, which is how it came to be that she met the handsome young cousin of the king— Morgan, Duke of Milton. But that is another story. . . .